Spreading Her Wings

Butterfly Princess Book 1

A Butterfly Princess sprang from her cozy chrysalis one morning in early spring. She had golden antennas like King Papa and lavender wings like Queen Mama, so they named her Laia.

As Laia yawned and stretched, her parents were both shocked to see a splash of scarlet like a fiery flame across her right lavender forewing.

"Swift Swallow will certainly see that mark!" Queen Mama said with a frown.

King Papa nodded. "Yes! And he will try to gobble our princess down!"

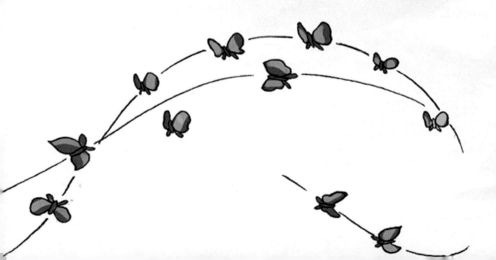

To: _____

From: _____

Day: _____

Alisa Hope Wagner is an award-winning author of Christian fiction and non-fiction books. She has a red birthmark on her right hand and arm.

You can find Alisa at her website: www.alisahopewagner.com and at her Facebook and Twitter: @alisahopewagner. Purchase her books on Amazon.

Albert Morales is an award-winning illustrator of comics, young adult fiction and children's books. He has a dark birthmark on his right hand.

You can contact Albert at artwise310@hotmail.com and find him on Instagram: @angryroosterstudios and Facebook: @albertmorales

Spreading Her Wings
Butterfly Princess Book 1
Marked Writers Publishing 2019
www.markedwriterspublishing.com
Written by Alisa Hope Wagner
Illustratated by Albert Morales
ISBN 13: 978-1-7334333-0-3
ISBN 10: 1-7334333-0-9

The King and Queen feared for their beautiful Butterfly Princess. They did not want Swift Swallow to see her scarlet flame and gulp her away. They pleaded with Laia to never spread her wings, for they loved her more than words could say.

"Yes, Papa and Mama," Laia said. "I will obey."

So the Butterfly Princess learned to keep her wings tightly bound. She hopped across leafy vines, so she would not be found.

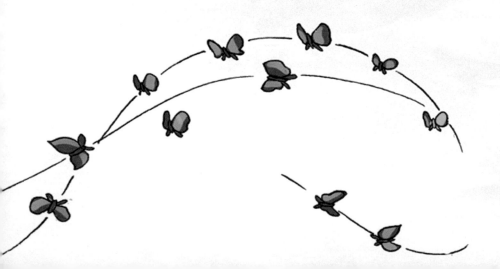

The Butterfly Princess grew up, and she would hide behind large green leaves and watch other butterflies float and flutter. She tiptoed along twisty twigs and broken branches as the butterfly friends played together.

But Laia always kept an attentive eye out for Swift Swallow with her wings folded in fear. She knew that if he spied her scarlet marking, he may try to fly near.

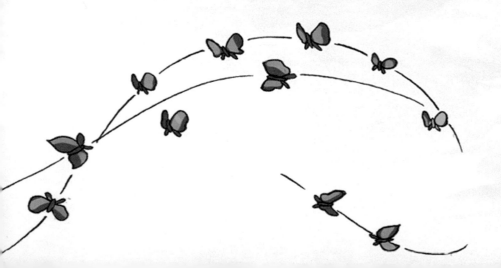

One day as the Butterfly Princess crept along the crevices of the woodlands, she saw a silhouette of something in the distance. It was Swift Swallow giving chase to his afternoon snack.

Although he was just as big as Laia had imagined, he didn't seem as fast as her parents had claimed. Swift Swallow quickly gave up the pursuit, and instead of lunch, he decided on a midday nap.

After he nestled in and closed his eyes, Laia decided to unfurl her wings. They ached from being securely clasped, and they longed for her to stretch them out and give a clap.

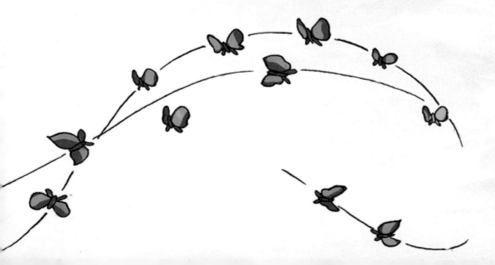

The Butterfly Princess went to inspect her right forewing, but she could not see the red mark well in the shadow. So she carefully edged to the end of the bent branch and into the brightness of the meadow.

Laia fretted for a moment, but she needed to know why the fiery flame across her lavender forewing worried her parents so.

"It is a wonder," she said with a pause, "but I rather like what I see. There is not a single butterfly in all the forest created to look like me."

Laia's gaze then turned toward the sunny scene, and she beheld the wavy green hills. She imagined her outstretched wings flying faster than Swift Swallow across the open fields.

"What do you say, Wind? Will you guide my lavender wings beyond the bendy branches and shady leaves?"

"How about you, Sun? Will you light a path for my golden antennas over the boundless grassy seas?"

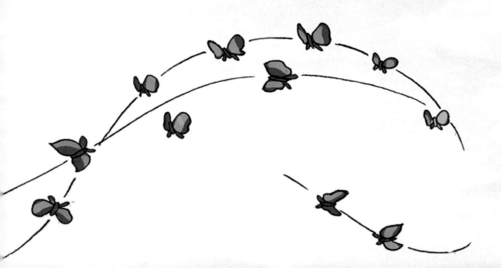

Laia's golden antennas glinted in the sun's radiant rays and her wings vibrated in the blissful breeze. She could no longer resist the urge to ascend above the confining trees.

The Butterfly Princess leapt over the shady shrubs where she spent her life hidden and afraid. Then she glided along a gentle gale, enjoying the whooshing sound her wings made.

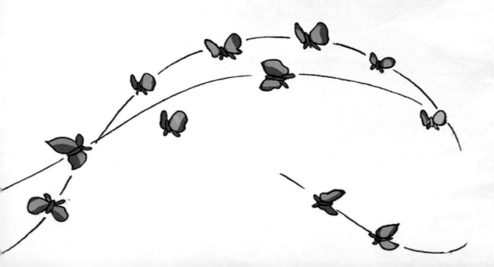

Unknowingly, the Butterfly Princess flew into her parents' view. King Papa quivered at the splendid sight of Laia sailing upon an airy stream. And Queen Mama fluttered with fascination at the brilliant hue on her daughter's right forewing.

Swift Swallow also noticed Butterfly Princess, but he did not stir from his steepled lair. He knew that he was no match for the scarlet, fiery flame that burned through the air.

Finally, the Butterfly Princess spotted King Papa and Queen Mama standing on a bowed branch stretching out from the forest rim. Laia's heart filled with joy, and she danced and flipped and waltzed and spun before landing lightly on a limb.

King Papa's golden antennas were lowered, and his embarrassment he could not hide. Queen Mama's lavender wings were folded and hanging sorrowfully to one side.

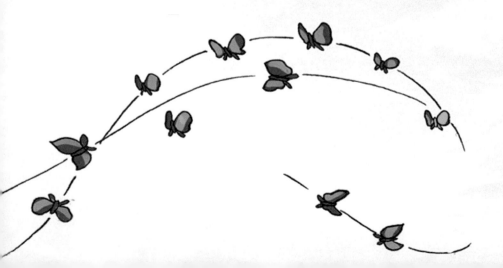

"What is wrong, Mama and Papa? Did you not see my fabulous flight?" the Butterfly Princess asked with concern.

"My golden antennas shone in the sun, and my lavender wings were not shut tight. I sliced through the warming air and soared around the sunlit sky. And, yes, Swift Swallow did stop and stare, but he did not choose to fly."

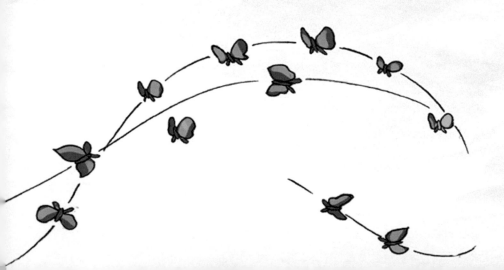

King Papa lifted his golden antennas and Queen Mama straightened her lavender wings.

"We are ashamed, our beautiful Butterfly Princess. We thought we were protecting you from Swift Swallow all this time. Now we realize that your marking is not a flaw. Instead, it is a glorious design."

Laia embraced King Papa and Queen Mama, and all was forgiven and made well. From now on, she no longer had to hide behind a thick, foresty veil.

Then Butterfly Princess smiled and turned her
golden antennas toward the sun-splashed meadow.
She unfurled her lavender wings and gave a giant
leap into the dazzling day.

Her fiery flame streaked across the sky, but Swift
Swallow dare not follow. And Laia knew that the
Wind would guide her and the Sun would light her
way.

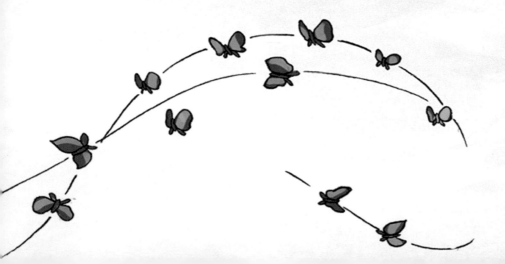

This story is dedicated to all who have been beautifully marked by birth or life.

Go fly in the uniqueness of your design.

"Thank you for making me so wonderfully complex!
Your workmanship is marvelous—how well I know it."
Psalm 139:14 (NLT)

Made in the USA
Lexington, KY
03 September 2019